PINKY and REX
and the
Just-Right Pet

PINKY and REX
and the
Just-Right Pet

by James Howe
illustrated by Melissa Sweet

READY-TO-READ

ALADDIN PAPERBACKS
NEW YORK LONDON TORONTO SYDNEY SINGAPORE

First Aladdin Paperbacks edition May 2002
Text copyright © 2001 by James Howe
Illustrations copyright © 2001 by Melissa Sweet

Aladdin Paperbacks
An imprint of Simon & Schuster
Children's Publishing Division
1230 Avenue of the Americas
New York, NY 10020

Also available in an Atheneum Books for Young Readers edition.
Printed and bound in the United States of America
6 8 10 9 7
Library of Congress Cataloging-in-Publication Data
Howe, James, 1946–
Pinky and Rex and the just right pet / by James Howe ;
illustrated by Melissa Sweet.—1st ed.
p. cm.— (Ready to read)
Summary: Seven-year-old Pinky, a confirmed dog lover, has a change of heart
after his family's new pet kitten pounces on his foot in the middle of the night.
ISBN 0-689-82861-6
[1. Pets—Fiction. 2. Cats—Fiction. 3. Animals—Infancy—Fiction.]
I. Sweet, Melissa, ill. II. Title. III. Series
PZ7.H83727 Pij 2001
[E]—dc21   00-026034
ISBN 978-0-689-83942-9 (Aladdin pbk.)
1209 LAK

To my grandniece, Amanda
—J. H.

To Sophie and Jack
—M. S.

Contents

Chapter 1

The Family Meeting

Pinky and Rex were in the middle of playing their favorite board game when Pinky noticed the time.

"Oh, no!" he said, jumping up. "I'm going to be late."

Rex glanced at the clock on her bedroom wall. "But if you leave now," she said, "I win."

"I know, but this is important. We're having a family meeting. We're going to decide about getting a pet."

"A pet? You'd better hurry, Pinky.

What if your mom and dad are letting Amanda decide without you?"

Pinky looked worried. "I don't think they'd do that . . . would they?" he asked.

Without waiting for an answer, he ran as quickly as he could to his house across the street.

"It's about time!" his little sister Amanda said. Their parents were sitting on either side of her at the kitchen table.

"Sorry I'm late," Pinky said.

"If you're more than five minutes late to a meeting, you lose your vote," said Amanda. "Forever."

Pinky sat down. "Then you've already lost your vote," he said, "because you were late last time."

Amanda glared at Pinky. "I was in the bathroom," she said.

"You were *singing* in the bathroom. I heard you."

"Not fair!" said Amanda. "Anyone who listens outside bathroom doors loses his vote!"

"Does not."

"Forever!"

"No way!"

"Amanda, Pinky!" their mother said firmly. "Enough. We have more important things to talk about. And *everyone* gets to vote."

"We need to decide, once and for all," their father said, "what kind of pet we want."

"A dog!" Pinky shouted.

"A cat!" Amanda cried.

"A problem," their mother said.

"How about a goldfish?" asked their father.

Chapter 2

The Plan

It was the next day and Pinky was not happy.

Amanda had voted for a cat. His mother had voted for a cat. Even his father, who had started out saying he wanted a dog, had voted for a cat. Only Pinky had voted for a dog. He had tried to vote twice, but Amanda said his vote didn't count even once because he had been late. *And* he listened at bathroom doors.

"My mom and dad said a dog would be too much work," Pinky told Rex. They were sitting on the front steps of Pinky's house, waiting to go with his father and Amanda to the supermarket.

"I told them I would take care of it," said Pinky. "I said I would feed it and walk it and clean up after it and everything."

"That sounds fair," Rex said.

Pinky shook his head. "That's not what my mom and dad think. They said it *wouldn't* be fair to expect me to do all that. I'm only seven, they said. But I really *want* a dog, Rex. Cats are okay, but they don't love you the way dogs do."

Rex nodded. "You're right," she said.

Pinky leaned toward Rex and whispered, "But I have a plan."

"What is it?" Rex whispered back.

"I think my dad really wants a dog more than a cat. So when we go to the animal shelter tomorrow, I'll find a really cute puppy and say, 'Hey, Dad, look at this!' All I have to do is get him to take one little look—and that puppy will be on its way home with me!"

Rex nodded seriously. "That's a good plan," she said as Pinky's father and

8

Amanda came out of the house and Amanda ran past them to the car.

Pinky scrambled into the car after Rex. "All I have to do is keep my fingers crossed until tomorrow," he told her softly. "And get Amanda to stop talking about kittens all the time."

As the car pulled away, Amanda said, "Another reason kittens are better is that they purr. Dogs don't purr. They

don't know how. *My* kitten is going to purr *all* the time!"

Pinky crossed all of his fingers. He put his hands in his lap and crossed his thumbs. "Puppy," he said under his breath. "Puppy, puppy."

But when his father pulled into a parking spot in front of the supermarket, Pinky knew that even if he could have crossed his toes as well as his fingers and thumbs, nothing was going to bring him luck.

"Look!" Amanda squealed.

There, right by the front door of the market, sat a girl next to a big cardboard box. On the side of the box it said:

FREE Kittens

By the time the others reached her, Pinky's little sister was already cuddling a tiny ball of black, white, and orange fur.

"Ook at dis iddle baby," she said. "Isn't it da cootest ting?"

"Dad, make Amanda stop," Pinky said. "I'm going to throw up."

But Pinky's father didn't hear him. He was too busy looking at the kitten himself.

"It *is* awfully cute," he said.

"She," the girl said. "The kitten is a she."

Pinky looked into the box. There were two short-haired black kittens, one of which had a spot of white on its tail. They were cute, but they weren't nearly as cute as the one Amanda held in her arms.

"Can I have her, Daddy?" Amanda pleaded. "Please?!"

She gazed up at her father with wide eyes. Pinky looked first at the kitten in his sister's arms, then at the expression on his father's face. Two by two, he uncrossed all his fingers and said good-bye to his plan.

And to his puppy.

Chapter 3
Patches

Amanda insisted that the kitten be named Patches.

She made a bed for her out of a box, an old pillow, and a towel.

"She will love this bed," Amanda informed Pinky as she plunked the kitten down into it.

Patches sniffed the towel, mewed, and climbed out.

"She will *learn* to love this bed," Amanda said, scooping the kitten up and plunking her back down into the bed.

This time, Patches didn't even bother sniffing before climbing out of the box.

Amanda's mother stood in the doorway. "Amanda," she said. "Remember, Patches belongs to everyone. She's the family's pet."

"I know that," said Amanda.

But as soon as her mother left the room, Amanda turned to Pinky and said, "She's really mine. I was the first one to hold her and that makes me her mother."

Pinky shrugged. "I don't care," he said.

"You shouldn't," said Amanda, giving Patches such a tight squeeze that the kitten squealed.

"Naughty kitty," Amanda said. "Don't you know I love you?"

"Maybe you shouldn't squeeze her so hard," Pinky suggested.

"I am not squeezing her hard," said Amanda. "I know how to squeeze a kitten. I am her mother, after all."

Pinky shook his head, got up, and left his sister's room. He winced as he heard the kitten squeal again.

That night, Pinky lay in bed thinking.
He was glad they had a pet, even if it
was only a kitten. He really didn't mind
that Amanda thought the kitten was
hers. He would have probably felt the
same way if they'd gotten a puppy. What
bothered him was that he hadn't even
had a *chance* to put his plan into
action. If only he had been able to get
his father to look at a puppy the way
he'd looked at that kitten, Pinky was

sure he could have convinced him to get a dog.

Pinky drifted off to sleep the same way he had many times before, picturing a dog lying at the foot of his bed. *His* dog.

Sometime in the middle of the night, he woke up with a start. Something was attacking his foot. In a rectangle of moonlight, he made out what the something was.

"Patches," he whispered, "what are you doing down there?"

The kitten jerked her head up and looked at him, her shiny, wet eyes glowing. Then she looked back at the bump under the covers, flattened her ears, wiggled her rear end, and pounced again.

Pinky couldn't help himself. He giggled.

Chapter 4

Pinky's Secret

Every night after that, the same thing happened. Patches would pounce on Pinky's foot. Pinky would wake with a start. The two of them would play until they both got sleepy. And then Patches would curl up in the curve of Pinky's shoulder and neck, purring so loudly that Pinky would have to say, "Hey,

Patches, how am I supposed to go back to sleep with your motor running right next to my ear?"

But he always smiled when he said it.

At first, Amanda had to be the one to feed Patches. But she got bored quickly.

"I'll feed her," Pinky said when he saw his father opening the bag of kitten food.

"Fine with me," said his father. He handed the bag to Pinky and nodded toward Patches, who was rubbing herself against Pinky's ankle. "Looks like you've got a friend."

Pinky smiled. "I guess," he said. Then putting a hand to the side of his mouth, he whispered, "She's not as good as a puppy, but she's okay. Don't tell her I said that."

Pinky's father nodded solemnly. "It will be our secret," he said.

It wasn't the secret he was keeping from Patches that bothered Pinky, however. It was the secret he was keeping from Amanda.

The next day, while Amanda was at a birthday party, Pinky and Rex decided to make a play house for Patches out of cardboard cartons and oatmeal-

container tubes. There were windows
for Patches to look out of, tunnels to
climb through, and old pieces of carpet
for scratching. When they were all
done, they took a big marker and wrote
on one side:

PATCHES' PLAY PALACE

Patches played in her palace for a long time. She loved it.

Rex noticed how Patches would play for a while, then run to Pinky for some cuddling before going back to play again.

"That is so cute," Rex said, when
Patches, finally worn out from her
playing, climbed up Pinky's shirt and
nestled into her favorite spot to fall
asleep. "She's so little she can sleep on
your shoulder. She really loves you."

Pinky raised his hand and gently stroked the kitten's back. It took him a moment to tell Rex what was bothering him.

"Amanda thinks that Patches is all hers," he told her. "But every night she comes into my room and sleeps in my bed. Amanda doesn't know. It's kind of a secret."

"Maybe Patches just likes you more," Rex said.

"Maybe," said Pinky, "but it isn't fair. Amanda wanted her more than I did. I don't care about a *cat*. I want a dog."

But that night, Pinky realized he was no longer picturing a dog lying at the foot of his bed as he drifted to sleep. He was picturing Patches curled up next to his ear. He could almost hear her purring.

Chapter 5

Gone!

Amanda didn't seem to notice that Patches rubbed up against Pinky's legs whenever she was hungry. She didn't notice that it was Pinky who had taken charge of cleaning out the kitten's litter box. She never asked why Patches was no longer in her room in the morning or where she had gone.

She just kept on picking Patches up,
squeezing her until the kitten squealed
and squirmed to get away, tried to
make her do things she didn't want to
do, and told her over and over again,
"You're my iddle kitty-cat."

Pinky stopped saying he was going
to throw up every time she talked like
that, but he didn't stop thinking it.

What he *did* say was, "You're too rough with her, Amanda. Be nice."

And Amanda always said, "I *am* nice, Pinky. You're just jealous because she's my cat."

"Am not," Pinky would say. But he began to wonder: Whose cat *is* she, anyway?

"Mom," Pinky said to his mother one day, "I think we should have two pets. Then Amanda and I could each have one."

Pinky's mother didn't say no. And she didn't say yes. She nodded her head slowly and said, "We'll have to think about that one, Pinky."

Later, Pinky found Rex in her front yard throwing a ball up in the air and playing catch with herself.

"When I'm a father," he told Rex,

"I'm never going to tell my kid, 'I'll
have to think about it.' You know why?"

"Why?" Rex asked. She had no idea
what Pinky was talking about.

"Because 'thinking about it' means
no!"

"Not always," said Rex. "My mom
and dad thought about adopting a
baby for a long time. And now we have
Matthew."

"That's different," Pinky said.

Just then, Amanda came running out of the house across the street.

"Pinky!" she shouted. "Patches is gone!"

Chapter 6

A Pet for Pinky

Rex ran with Pinky to join in the hunt for the missing kitten.

"We've looked everywhere already!" Amanda cried. "I keep calling her name, but there isn't any answer. Do you think she's dead, Pinky?"

"Now, Amanda," their father said, "you've already asked us that. And we've told you she is *not* dead, she is probably just hiding someplace."

While Pinky's parents searched upstairs, Pinky and Rex and Amanda searched downstairs and outside. Pinky felt confident he'd find her. After all, he had come to know that kitten pretty well.

"Patches! Patches, where are you?" he called. But there was no answer.

Hours passed. And still there was no sign of Patches.

"She's dead!" Amanda wailed as she got ready for bed.

"If she doesn't show up by the morning," her father said, "we'll make flyers and put them up around town."

Amanda's mother went to sit with Amanda while she tried to fall asleep.

Pinky went to bed by himself—or so he thought.

No sooner had he stretched his legs out under the covers than his foot touched something soft and warm and fuzzy. The something moved. The something had a tongue, and the tongue licked and tickled the bottom of Pinky's foot.

"Patches!" Pinky cried.

He could feel the kitten climbing up his leg, over his belly and chest, until suddenly there she was, poking her head out from under the covers, her eyes looking right into his. She yawned and then began to give his nose a bath.

"Oh, Patches," Pinky said.

Amanda and her mother appeared at the door.

"We heard you shout," their mother said.

"You found her!" Amanda cried gleefully. "You found her!" She jumped on Pinky's bed and rubbed her face against Patches' fur.

"She found *me*," said Pinky.

"You can hear that purring from the next room," said their father, joining them. "So where was she?"

"In my bed," said Pinky. Turning to the kitten, he said, "Yes, you were. And you had everybody worried, didn't you, you naughty little kitty-witty."

Amanda said, "I'm going to throw up."

Everyone laughed.

Pinky's mother sat down on the edge of the bed. "Pinky," she said, "Daddy and I have been talking. You've shown a lot of responsibility taking care of Patches. We think you should have a pet of your own. Maybe even a dog. Someday. Maybe soon."

"But—"

"I know, I know, you'd like a pet *now*. But we want to wait just a little longer. Getting used to one animal around the house is enough."

"I wasn't going to say that," said Pinky. "I was going to say I wasn't sure I even want a dog anymore. I kind of, well, I think I like cats more."

Pinky's mother smiled.

"Anyway, Pinky already has a pet," said Amanda.

"I do?" Pinky asked.

"Well, you *are* her father, for heaven's sake," said Amanda. "You don't expect me to do *everything* for her, do you? Oh, and since you found her, I guess maybe I'll let her stay in here with you tonight."

With that said, she kissed Patches on the top of her head, took her mother by the hand, and bounced off to her own bedroom.

Watching her go, Pinky's father shook his head. "Amanda is full of surprises," he said. "But even she can see how good you are with that kitten, Pinky. Patches is lucky to have a dad like you."

Pinky blushed. He didn't know what to say.

But Patches did. She turned her motor up, purring loudly in Pinky's ear, letting him know that his father was right.